Our Fat Cat

by Wendy Blaxland

Illustrated by
Shirley Peters

CAMBRIDGE
UNIVERSITY PRESS
www.cambridge.org

Where is our fat cat?

Is she on her mat?

Is she having a nap?

We called and called

our fat cat.

We tapped her bowl.

Then Dad called us

from the van.

Our cat wasn't fat

any more!